Fuss on the Bus

'Fuss on the Bus'
An original concept by Heather Pindar
© Heather Pindar

Illustrated by Angelika Scudamore

Published by MAVERICK ARTS PUBLISHING LTD
Studio 3A, City Business Centre, 6 Brighton Road,
Horsham, West Sussex, RH13 5BB
© Maverick Arts Publishing Limited August 2018
+44 (0)1403 256941

A CIP catalogue record for this book is available at the British Library.

ISBN 978-1-84886-367-5

www.maverickbooks.co.uk

This book is rated as: Blue Band (Guided Reading)
This story is decodable at Letters and Sounds Phase 4/5.

Fuss on the Bus

by **Heather Pindar**
illustrated by **Angelika Scudamore**

Everyone was waiting for Sid's bus.

"You can get on," said Sid, "But..."

"...NO FUSS on MY BUS!"

"Yes, Sid," said Camel.

"Yes, Sid," said the monkeys.

"Yes, Sid," said Duck.

"Yes, Sid," said the children.

"Good," said Sid. "No fuss.

Off we go!"

11

"OW!" said Duck.

"Camel, you are squishing us!"

Click-clack!

Click-clack!

6   TOWN

The monkeys went up
onto the roof.

13

Thump, thump, thump!

The children ran up and down.

"Quack!" said Duck.

"No fuss on my bus!" said Sid.

Everyone sat still.

Everyone was quiet.

"Good," said Sid.

"That's better. No fuss."

"Chick-a-boom, chick-a-boom, chick-a-boom!" sang the children.

"Quack!" said Duck.

Tap, tap, tap went the monkeys
on the roof.

"No fuss on my bus!" said Sid.

"Get off! All of you!"

Sid zoomed off.

Bang!

A wheel fell off the bus!

"This bus is too much fuss!" said Sid.

"Chick-a-boom...

It was Camel, with everyone on top.

"Hop on, Sid!" said Camel.

"Chick-a-boom, chick-a-boom,
chick-a-boom!" sang Sid.

"Yippee!" he said, "This is
much better than my bus!"

Quiz

1. What is there on Sid's bus?
a) No eating
b) No fuss
c) No waiting

2. Who is squishing everyone?
a) Camel
b) Cow
c) Monkeys

3. Where do the monkeys go?
a) To the toilet
b) At the back
c) On the roof

4. What do the children sing?

a) Choo-choo!

b) Wizz-pop!

c) Chick-a-boom!

5. What happens to the bus?

a) A wheel falls off

b) The horn breaks

c) The windows fall off

Turn over for answers

Book Bands for Guided Reading

The Institute of Education book banding system is a scale of colours that reflects the various levels of reading difficulty. The bands are assigned by taking into account the content, the language style, the layout and phonics.

Maverick Early Readers are a bright, attractive range of books covering the pink to purple bands. All of these books have been book banded for guided reading to the industry standard and edited by a leading educational consultant.

To view the whole Maverick Readers scheme, visit our website at

www.maverickearlyreaders.com

Or scan the QR code above to view our scheme instantly!

Quiz Answers: 1b, 2a, 3c, 4c, 5a